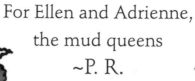
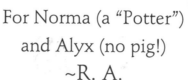

For Ellen and Adrienne,
the mud queens
~P. R.

For Norma (a "Potter")
and Alyx (no pig!)
~R. A.

First edition 1996

Library of Congress Cataloging-in-Publication Data

Root, Phyllis.
Mrs. Potter's pig / Phyllis Root ; illustrated by Russell Ayto. — 1st ed.
Summary: Mrs. Potter keeps everything perfectly clean, except for her baby daughter
Ermajean, who delights in being so messy that she seems to turn into a pig.
ISBN 1-56402-924-7
[1. Orderliness — Fiction. 2. Babies — Fiction. 3. Pigs — Fiction.]
I. Ayto, Russell, ill. II. Title.
PZ7.R6784Mr   1996
[E] — dc20   95-38194

2 4 6 8 10 9 7 5 3 1

This book was typeset in Stempel Schneidler.
The pictures were done in watercolor and ink.

Printed in Hong Kong

Candlewick Press
2067 Massachusetts Avenue
Cambridge, Massachusetts 02140

Mrs. Potter's Pig

Phyllis Root

illustrated by
Russell Ayto

CANDLEWICK PRESS
CAMBRIDGE, MASSACHUSETTS

Mrs. Potter kept a spotless house. The windows glistened. The floors glowed.

She even dusted the chickens until they squawked.

Everything in Mrs. Potter's house was swept and washed and polished and mopped perfectly clean.

Everything except
baby Ermajean.
Ermajean
loved mess.

She drooled
and gurgled
on her white
ruffled dresses.

After every
meal, she had
applesauce
behind her ears.

And any speck of dirt
in the yard clung to
baby Ermajean
like bees to clover.

"Ermajean," complained Mrs. Potter,
"you're as dirty as a little pig.
Someday, if you're not careful,
you'll turn into one."

Ermajean even sounded like a pig.

She did not coo and babble like other babies.

She snorted and snuffled when she slept.

She gurgled and grunted while she ate.

One sunny day
Mrs. Potter
tucked Ermajean
into her buggy,
gave her a
rice cake, and
wheeled her out
into the yard to
get some sun.

"Now sit here and stay clean," Mrs. Potter told Ermajean. And off she went to dust the picket fence.

But Ermajean soon got bored.
Clutching her rice cake,
she crawled out of the buggy
and across the lawn,
leaving a trail of crumbs
behind her.

Straight through the loose board in the
pigpen fence crawled baby Ermajean—
smack into the middle of the biggest, muddiest
puddle she could find. Ermajean squealed
with joy and dropped her rice cake in the mud.
A little piglet came and gobbled it up . . .

He followed the trail
of rice cake crumbs
through the loose board
in the pigpen fence,
across the lawn, and straight
up into the baby buggy.

Mrs. Potter dusted
the last picket on
the fence and stretched
her arms in the sun.
"What a fine day,"
she said to herself.
"I'll just take baby
Ermajean for a stroll
before I wax
the weathervane
on the barn."

She peeked into the buggy. Little snorts came from a bump under the blanket. *How sweet,* thought Mrs. Potter, *baby Ermajean is sleeping.*

Snort! Snort!

She wheeled the buggy out through the gate and down the road.

"This road could use a little sweeping," she said to herself. The buggy bounced and bumped and woke the piglet up. "*Snort,*" said the piglet under the blanket.

"The lilacs look a little dusty," Mrs. Potter remarked. "*Snuffle*," said the piglet as it rooted for more rice cake crumbs.

"The trees could use some sprucing up," said Mrs. Potter. "*Grunt*," said the piglet. It poked its snout from under the blanket.

She snatched the piglet out of the buggy and hugged it tight. "Don't worry, Ermajean," she comforted the baby pig.

Back up the road she raced to call the doctor and see what could be done.

"Come back, Ermajean!" Mrs. Potter cried. She sprinted to the pigpen . . .

As she opened the gate, the piglet squirmed free and ran toward the loose board in the pigpen fence.

. . . and there,
in the mud,
sat baby Ermajean.
"Oh, Ermajean, thank
goodness
you're
yourself
again!" cried
Mrs. Potter.
"Come out of
there this instant!"

Ermajean squealed
and clutched
a fistful of mud.
"Come out right now!"
ordered Mrs. Potter.
"Or I shall have to
come and get you."
Ermajean dug her
toes into the mud
and snorted
with glee.

Mrs. Potter sighed. She took off her shoes and socks and climbed over the pigpen fence.

Squooze oozed the mud between her toes. "Oh," said Mrs. Potter in surprise.

Shloop squelched the mud around her heels. "Why," said Mrs. Potter, "this feels . . . nice."

She squoozed and
shlooped her way
over to baby
Ermajean, picked
her up, and hugged
her hard, mud and all.

"Ermajean," said Mrs. Potter, "you are a pig. A happy little mud pig." Ermajean shrieked happily and plastered her mother's nose with mud. Right there in the pigpen Mrs. Potter and Ermajean tromped and stomped and splashed.

Mrs. Potter still keeps
a spotless house.
The doorknobs gleam.
The copper pots shine.
She even scrubs the garbage
before she throws it away.

But on sunny afternoons
Mrs. Potter and
Ermajean slip away
to the pigpen . . .

. . . take off
their shoes, and dance
a messy mud jig
together.